To the beloved
Laith and Kaiden

زين

The Birds and The Key

© Copyright 2020 Therese Basha
About the book and the art

All art is original by Therese Basha

For more information on Therese Basha art
Contact: Tata254@gmail.com
www.ThereseBashaArt.com

ACKNOWLEDGEMENT

Many thanks go to all the people who love art and support me in all the journeys I undertake.

Special gratitude goes to my creative writing instructor, Jas Obrecht; my supportive husband, Ibrahim; and my family.

I will be remiss if I don't thank the "frowning cashier" whose un-kind treatment inspired me to write this story.

Keep smiling. Be kind and make somebody's day! "Peace begins with a smile." Mother Teresa

DEDICATION

To my everything, my daughters, Nada and Marian.

In a beautiful small house lived a family of birds.

Some were boys and some were girls. All were brothers and sisters.

The eldest was named Ideas, the second Pens, the third Letters, and the fourth Wires.

The fifth was named Feelings and last but not least, the sixth had the name Memory.

Memory always dreamed of tomorrow.

A giant bird guarded the door to the siblings' house.

Whenever it was sunny, the giant bird's wings spread apart to shade the little ones from the strong sun rays.

She cared for them and wanted them to feel comfortable and safe.

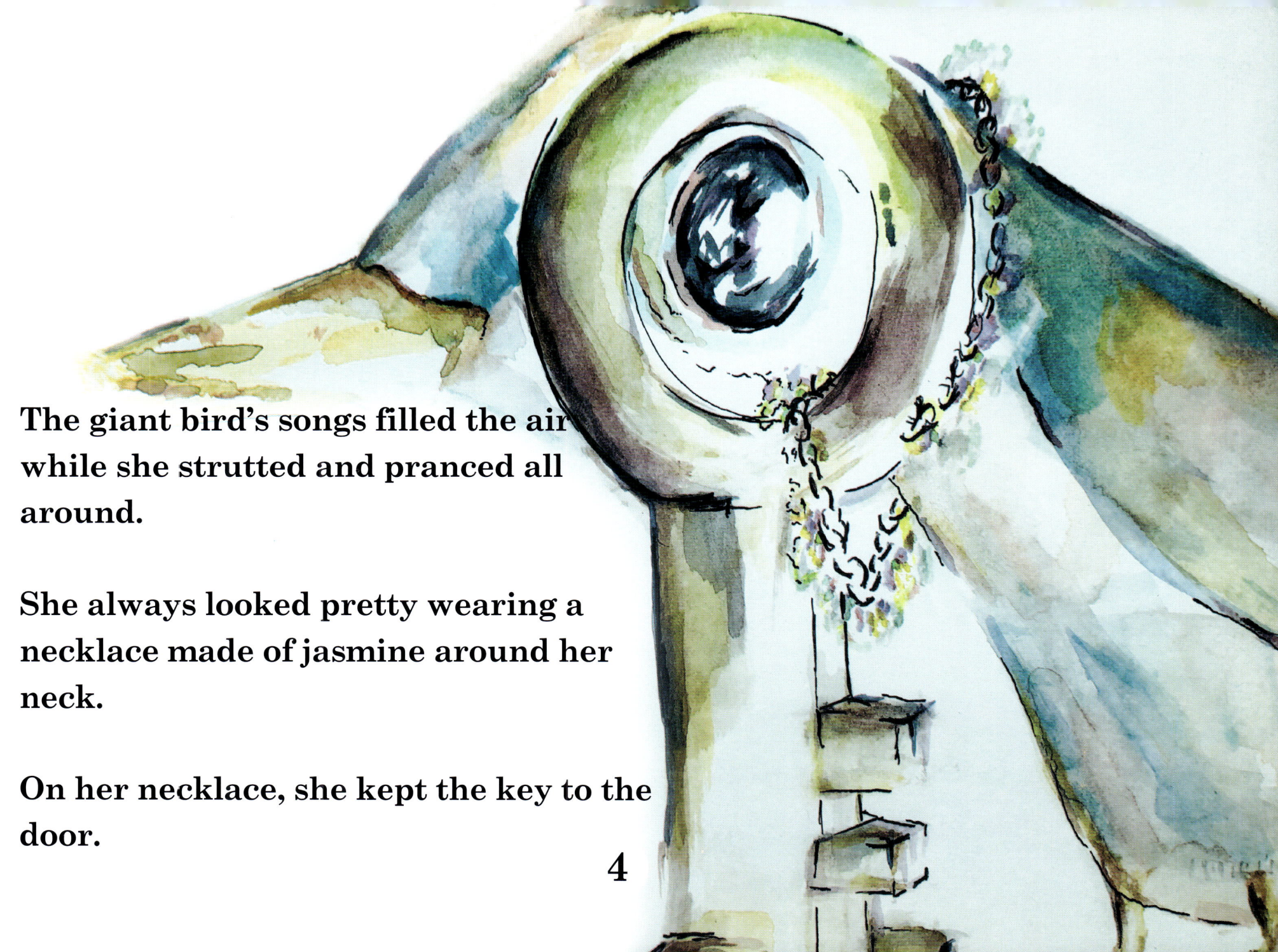

The giant bird's songs filled the air while she strutted and pranced all around.

She always looked pretty wearing a necklace made of jasmine around her neck.

On her necklace, she kept the key to the door.

One sunny morning, Ideas wanted to go out to play.

As usual, he needed to call the giant bird to unlock the door.

He loudly began to call: "S... S... S... S... S...."

"Darn," he thought. "I can't remember the giant's name!"

"O giant, giant, I am Ideas, the one who helps you think."

Struggling, he started to wander around the room, talking to himself and hoping to remember.

After a while, he thought, "Stop it. Don't tire yourself.

The moon's gonna come out, the day's gonna be over, and you will not remember."

Still, he persevered in his attempts and hurried to ask his brothers and sisters.

Pens got up from sleep and left behind all his dreams. With a pen, he attempted to write the name, hoping against hope to remember.

"S… S… S… S! For the life of me,
I can't remember.

Back to my dreams I go."
Off to sleep he went.

Lovely Letters tried to help her brother remember the giant's name and began to go over what she learned in school.

"A... B... C... I also can't remember," she said.

Angry, she got out all of her books and tried to solve this puzzle, until she remembered that today was her day off and her chance to rest – no homework, no thinking, no work.

Wires searched and searched. He looked at Twitter and WhatsApp.

He searched on Facebook and looked through his emails, trying to find the giant bird's name, but no luck.

He gave up and started singing to pass the time,

"Ring, ring…. My telephone is ringing.

Ring, ring….
No answer!
I keep singing.

I talk and sing all the time…for every word I can find a rhyme.

Ring, sing… Sing, ring."

Feelings, their sweet sister, went to see what was going on.

Her brothers' and sisters' nerves frayed. They were all upset and tangled up inside.

With a voice as sweet as honey, she tried to calm them and told them not to worry, since tomorrow is another day and they will play.

"Come out to play," shouted their friends Farouk, Merie, Maria, Nada, and Marian.

"We are outside waiting for you. Come on, come out."

Memory, the youngest of them all, sat in despair.

She could not remember the giant's name.

She had no idea how to figure it out. She knew that she had very little experience, which would not help her at all.

Quietly, she carried a book in her hands. With love and attention, she flipped the pages.

Between the folds, she found a beautiful rose.

Memory got excited.

She kissed the rose, and suddenly, its soft petals exuded a lovely fragrance. Its stem began to sway and the leaves danced as if following the melody of a beautiful song.

The red rose appeared as a shy full moon with a wide smile on its velvety cheeks.

Memory called her brothers and sisters and shouted, "Look, look, how beautiful!

The rose has a smile."

At once, the giant bird turned around and stopped singing..

"Smile! Who calls my name?" She asked.

Everyone got excited. Finally, they remembered the giant's name.

With joy, Smile, the giant bird, opened the door for them all to go out and play.

Hooray!

The End